Something Borrowed

A CLEAN INCLUSIVE ROMANCE

THE WEDDING TRIO
BOOK TWO

DAISY LANDISH

Editing by Rachael Lammie
Cover by Daisy Landish

BEACHES AND TRAILS
PUBLISHING

About the Author

Daisy Landish is a romance and contemporary fiction author living in the UK, whose clean and sweet novellas have tugged at readers' heartstrings across the pond and beyond. When she's not writing love stories, Daisy spends her time reading, hiking at dawn, and riding into the sunset on her horse, Rosebud.

Join Daisy's Newsletter for updates and giveaways!

f facebook.com/daisylandishromance

X x.com/daisy_landish

instagram.com/beachesandtrailspublishing

a amazon.com/author/daisylandish

BB bookbub.com/authors/daisy-landish

g goodreads.com/Daisy_Landish

Also by Daisy Landish

Clean Regency Romance

The Lady Series - The Allington Collection

The Lady Series - The Gillingham Collection

The Lady Series - The Blackmore Collection

The Lady Series - The Norrington Collection

Clean Contemporary Romance

Love on Spruce Island

Second Chance

Cherry Tree Island

The Wedding Trio

Extra Credit

Counting on the Cowboy

Focusing on the Cowboy

Mistletoe Magic

Cozy Mysteries

Jane and Kennedy Daniels Mysteries

Pine Grove Mysteries

Annie Archer Paranormal Mysteries

Wilma Wade Holiday Mysteries

Mike and Maddie Mysteries

Mystic Moonhaven Mysteries

Sweater Weather: Cozy Mysteries for Fall

Summer Vibes: Cozy Mysteries for Summer

One

AVERY SAT on the edge of the bed, looking at the closet and the chaos that was once the bedroom she shared with Gemma. Coat hangers lay discarded on the floor. Drawers slanted, impossible to close. The whole place was a mess. Avery let her tears fall. How had everything fallen apart so quickly? Gemma and Avery always had issues, but didn't everyone? Wasn't a small amount of conflict what kept life interesting? It kept the mind sharp and brought what was important into focus. That's what Avery had always told herself anyway.

Her wedding dress lay crumpled in the corner on the floor. Gemma had no regard for Avery's feelings when she'd discarded the dress so callously. Looking over at the nightstand, Avery caught a glimpse of the gold photo frame of her wedding day. Gemma and Avery in matching dresses stood side by side. It was taken only three years ago. When did it all go wrong?

She wondered if it had anything to do with the struggle they'd had trying to adopt their daughter, Emma. Being not only a same-sex couple but with one mother being trans-gender, it had been difficult. But Avery and Gemma never let that stop them. They pushed on, comforting each other through each rejection and celebrating with each piece of good news. Every tear had been worth it when they'd brought their little bundle of joy home.

"It was meant to be. A child who needed to be loved, finding a home with so much love to give," Gemma had said.

Thinking back to that day tore Avery's heart. Was it her or the baby that Gemma had issues with? Avery didn't want to give it a second thought. She had known Gemma had been unhappy for a while but assumed it was nothing more than her adjusting to her new life as a mother. Everything had been so beautiful, but once the novelty of a new baby wore off and responsibility kicked in, Gemma seemed to crumble.

She hadn't coped well with the sleepless nights and never knew how to handle Emma when she cried seemingly for no reason. She'd missed her old life of partying and freedom too much. When they argued one evening and Gemma threatened to leave, Avery never thought Gemma had meant it. *Just angry words meant to hurt,* she told herself. Little did Avery know just how much those words could hurt until she came home from a day out with Emma to find Gemma had packed her things and gone. No note, no explanation, nothing.

Emma crying from her bassinet in the living room broke Avery out of her self-pity. She didn't have the time to spill tears over someone who didn't deserve them. She had someone far more important to worry about. Her daughter needed her. Striding into the living room, Avery wiped away her tears and scooped up her beautiful four-month-old with a head full of dark curly hair and stunning emerald-green eyes. Looking at her child's face made her pain and worries melt away.

Emma had brought a new kind of love into Avery's life, a love like no other. She was a beacon of pure light. Avery would melt whenever she held her. When Emma looked up, and her lips creased into the closest thing to a smile a baby could manage, it was as though a light came on in the world. As long as she had Emma in her life, all was good and well.

"Don't you worry, baby, mommy is here. Everything will be okay," Avery said, swaying with Emma back and forth.

After giving Emma her bottle and putting her back to sleep, Avery had a small glass of wine to calm her nerves. Looking in the mirror, she gave herself a pep talk that she had memorized over the years.

You have fought through worse than this. You have come back from worse than this. You deserve love, and you are love. You are strong. You are beautiful, and the world is yours for the taking. It's ok to cry and be sad, but once you have cried your river, it's time to get back on the horse and slay.

It did the trick every time. With her pep talk ringing in her ears, Avery began to pick up the mess Gemma had left behind, boxing up old memories that only brought hurt and pain. She would call it a spring cleaning. Tidying up always helped Avery clear her mind. *Clearing out the negative energy only leaves room for the positive,* she told herself.

As the weeks went by, Avery thought that she was coping well until, one morning, she woke up to find a large yellow envelope waiting for her in the mailbox. She discarded it on the dining table, concentrating instead on fussing over Emma; she was in need of a diaper change. Envelopes like that never carried good news, and Avery was afraid of what might be inside. She busied herself with the task of settling the baby, fussing over little details that could probably be left for later. But the envelope screamed at her every time she caught a glimpse of it or passed by the table as she straightened the room. Eventually, she decided enough was enough. How bad could it be?

"Divorce papers?" Avery yelled, her voice waking Emma so that the baby cried. "She filed for divorce?"

A small part of Avery always thought Gemma would come back. That her act of rebellion was just her version of a mid-life crisis, and once it was out of her system, they would be a family again. As the large black letters stared back at her from the page, she felt the world around her crumble.

Avery was never one for self-pity, so she decided enough was enough. After a week of not leaving the house, it was time to take positive action. It wasn't just Gemma leaving that had left her feeling unsettled. It was the world around her. Her neighbours hadn't been the nicest when Gemma and Avery moved in. And she was tired of the general feel of the neighbourhood. Gemma's friends had become her friends, so she had no one when Gemma left. Apart from Emma, nothing was keeping her in that town anymore. She had only moved there because Gemma wanted to, Avery would have been happy to say in

Seattle. She didn't want Emma to be raised in a place that no longer held any love. What she needed was a new home. A fresh start.

It didn't take her long to find the small town called Summershore; a small town in the hills of California. It was perfect. It had a lovely lake, scenic views, and everything that Avery missed about home. Summershore called to her. With Emma on her hip, she left three days later to view a small little house she had spotted online.

Seeing it in person, Avery instantly fell in love. The picture didn't do the house justice. It was a cute two-storey building with a tiny front porch just big enough for a small porch swing. It had a dark grey door and roof, giving the house a cosy feel. The door opened up right into the living room. It had a cute cottage-style kitchen and two small bedrooms. It was just big enough for Avery and Emma.

"What do you think, sweetie? Is this the house for us?" Avery asked Emma.

Emma blinked back, not understanding the question, but Avery never honestly expected an answer.

She smiled at the realtor. "We'll take it!"

Her next adventure had begun.

Two

AFTER SETTING herself and Emma up in their new home, Avery spent a day strolling around Summershore in the afternoon sun, getting acquainted with her new hometown. Avery fell more in love with each welcoming hello, friendly smile, and scenic view and knew that Summershore would be the best home for herself and Emma.

"I think this place will be perfect for us," Avery rocked Emma to sleep on the porch swing. "But there is only so long I can chill. Mommy's got to get herself a job to give you all the best things in life."

Settling Emma down after her bottle, Avery loaded up her laptop, printed off some fresh copies of her resume, and began searching for job openings online. Many good jobs were just outside of Summershore, but the working hours would have been a conflict for a single mother. She needed a job with sociable hours, good pay, and something close to home to be there for Emma when she needed her. After several hours of searching, she submitted several applications. To her delight, she was able to set up several interviews over the next few days.

First was a marketing assistant position at Summershore's biggest marketing company. But they went with a candidate that had a little more knowledge of the area than Avery. She appreciated their communication. It vexed Avery when companies said that they would be in touch and then never followed through. Waiting was the worst. Her following interview was for a sales associate, and her third was for a catering assistant – Avery had always had a talent when it came to creating delicious meals in the kitchen.

After several weeks, Avery's confidence took a hit. While some interviews went well, nothing ever came of them, and others never even gave her a chance. She didn't want to think about why they rejected her, but based on her experience, she knew not everyone was open-minded when they realised she was trans, or compassionate to her needs as a new mother. As discouraging as it was, Avery had a thick skin and wouldn't let people get to her like that. Every morning before she left for another interview, she gave herself a pep talk, practised her power poses from her favourite positive mindset books and went out ready to take on the world.

"Crap, my savings hasn't taken a hit like this in years," she mumbled at the ATM as she withdrew funds to buy groceries.

After several weeks and no real sign of a job on the horizon, Avery began to panic. She had enough savings to last a bit longer, but she didn't want to rely on that. Her savings were dwindling quickly, and she had no idea what she would do once those funds ran out.

Avery headed to The Golden Coffee Bean to grab an iced Frappuccino where she came across a notice board. Scanning through the listings, she noticed several postings for jobs in the area. Some were less than ideal, with part-time hours or minimum wage. At this point, she decided she couldn't be picky. A job was a job, after all. One listing stuck out more than most. The poster was beautiful, and when she pulled off the tab with the contact details, butterflies fluttered in her stomach.

"*Love & Joy*, how cute," Avery murmured as she examined the logo at the top of the poster.

Avery sipped her Frappuccino and began to make calls, sitting outside where she could draw positive energy from the view of the lake and the rolling hills beyond. One vacancy had already been filled, and another had wrapped up the interview stage. She left *Love & Joy* until last. She didn't have a lot of management experience, but she thought the worst thing that could happen would be for them to say no. If she didn't try, what was she going to do? Sit around and wonder what might have happened?

Someone picked up on the first ring. "Good afternoon, Love & Joy Wedding and Event Planning. Dante speaking, how may I help you?" came a deep melodic voice.

"Hi, my name is Avery Lannister. I came across your advertisement for an assistant manager. Is the position still open?"

"Of course, of course. Do you have a pen? I'll give you our email address. Send over a copy of your resume and a cover letter detailing a little about yourself, and I will get back to you ASAP. We are scheduling interviews shortly, so the quicker you send it, the better. I'm not going to lie. We have had a lot of applicants so far," Dante replied.

Avery thanked him and jotted down the email on the napkin that came with her croissant. Not wanting to waste a second, she hung up and headed home with Emma to apply.

Three days later, Avery sat with her morning coffee on the front porch feeling defeated. She had no interviews lined up and debated applying for jobs outside of Summershore. She didn't want to hire a nanny to raise Emma, but what choice would she have if a job didn't present itself? A stray tear rolled down her cheek just as her phone rang. Wiping away her tear, she picked up her phone. It was a number she didn't recognize, but it was a local area code calling, from what she could tell. *A job?*

Her hands shook in anticipation making it hard to hit the button to accept the call. "Hello?"

"Hi, is this Avery Lannister?"

"It sure is. How can I help you?"

"It's Dante, from *Love & Joy*. You applied for the assistant manager position. While you don't have much management experience, your resume is impressive, and I'd love to invite you in for an interview." The happiness in Dante's voice was infectious, instantly lifting Avery's mood.

"Oh my god, thank you so much. When would you like me to come in?"

"Is Thursday or Friday better for you?"

"Friday gives me enough time to find a babysitter."

"Perfect, I will email you all the details. I look forward to meeting you. Enjoy your day." Dante ended the call.

Ecstatic, Avery jumped up and spent the next few hours hunting for a babysitter and planning her outfit, makeup, and shoes. She even spent time practising her interview skills in the bedroom mirror. She had an excellent feeling about *Love & Joy*, a feeling she hadn't had for a long time.

Friday rolled around. Her interview was scheduled for late afternoon, giving her enough time to get through her to-do list and care for Emma. Avery was ready to go, settling for a black power suit with a white and red polka dot shirt. Checking her watch, she began to worry that she would be late for the interview if her babysitter didn't turn up soon. First impressions were everything, and she didn't want to miss an excellent opportunity. Picking up her phone, she dialled the number for the agency she booked her babysitter through. Straight away, they patched her through to the young girl's phone.

"Hi, is this Stephanie? I have a booking with you to watch Emma for a couple of hours? I'm due to leave any minute. I was just wondering, what is your ETA?" Avery asked, trying to keep the nerves from her voice.

"I'm so sorry; I lost your number. I meant to call sooner. I won't be able to make it, something has come up at home, and I have to cancel all of my afternoon appointments," the girl replied and ended the call before Avery could even speak.

"Are you kidding? How unprofessional," Avery snapped, shoving her phone into her handbag.

Checking her watch, she had to think fast. If she didn't leave within five minutes, she wouldn't make it across town during rush hour traffic.

"Looks like you're coming with me," Avery smiled, scooping up Emma and heading to the car.

She arrived at *Love & Joy* with minutes to spare. Pulling her frontal baby carrier from the trunk, she strapped Emma to her chest, repeated her pep talk in her head, and strolled into the store with as much confidence as she could muster.

Three

A SMALL BELL rang above her head as she entered *Love & Joy*. Looking at the store, Avery was awestruck. It was beautiful, decorated in shades of pink and pale blue. A large canvas sat on the back wall behind the main desk depicting a wedding day and a couple with a baby boy in their arms. Flowers sat on every table, the scent a delight to the senses. Avery felt her skin break out into goosebumps like it did when she first saw her new home.

A tall, dark, handsome, and very well-dressed man greeted her with a warm and welcoming smile. He had impeccable style, and Avery couldn't help but admire him.

"Hello, how can we help you? Are you here to organize a party for this little darling?" he asked, stroking Emma on the cheek. He shook her hand and led her over to the small area with 'Consultation' written in gold calligraphy on the wall.

"No, actually, I'm here for the interview. I'm Avery Lannister. I'm so sorry my babysitter cancelled last minute, and I didn't want to miss such a wonderful opportunity," Avery smiled nervously, sitting down and unbuckling Emma's carrier.

"Not a problem at all, would you like a drink?" offered a tall blonde-haired beauty as she joined them from the other side of the room. Avery had caught a glimpse of the woman's picture around the store when she entered, quickly realizing she was Juliette, the owner.

Avery smiled. "No, thank you."

She didn't know if it was the beauty of the story, the goosebumps she felt when she walked in, or the welcoming atmosphere, but she felt instantly at ease as they told her a little about what they did at *Love & Joy*. She got a feeling of being home and knew in her heart that she could be herself with them. She decided honesty was the best policy and explained that while she didn't have much experience, she was a quick study and always willing to learn. She listed her prior experience in sales and customer service.

"I'm looking for a job that will allow me the freedom to still have a hand in raising my daughter.... I don't want her to be raised by a nanny." This was the deal-breaker, and she knew it. Not many companies would be so understanding of this goal. Avery sat waiting, her heart pounding at the surprise on their faces.

The surprise didn't last before their faces broke into smiles, instantly putting Avery at ease. After the standard interview questions, Dante excused himself to check on Avery's references leaving her and Juliette to talk. Juliette was so open and kind that Avery felt free to tell her story. She gave her a brief outline of how she and Gemma adopted Emma and how Gemma left. She didn't feel the need to hide the fact she was transgender and appreciated how Juliette listened and took it all in. Juliette was a mother herself, so she understood Avery's need to be in her daughter's life, not wanting to miss out on the milestones.

"I hear you. Thank you for sharing your story," Juliette smiled, placing a comforting hand on Avery's knee. "So is Avery your legal name...did you..."

Avery smiled sweetly, she could tell Juliette was a caring person and didn't want to upset or offend her, but these questions need to be asked when filling out the documentation for hiring someone new. She had to do what was right for her business.

"It's okay, you can ask. Avery is my birth name. It was like my parents knew I would need a gender-neutral name later on in life."

Juliette beamed. "That's beautiful. I love that."

Dante re-joined them. The rest of the interview didn't last much longer before Dante and Juliette, after a quick consultation, offered Avery the job on the spot. Overjoyed, Avery had to stop herself from crying tears of joy. She was so excited that she didn't want to wait until the following week and insisted she could start right away.

Juliette agreed that Avery was more than welcome to bring Emma into the office with her if a babysitter wasn't possible, making Avery even happier. She was super grateful for her understanding and wanted to thank her by doing the best job she possibly could. Avery felt like she fit into the team instantly. It was like she was meant to find *Love & Joy* in order to restore the love and joy in her own life.

Juliette and Dante gave Avery a list of responsibilities to choose from. Given that she didn't have much experience, they didn't want to overwhelm her with tasks she couldn't handle. With her sales and customer service background, Avery jumped at the chance to manage the new client accounts and took over opening the newly extended part of the store. She worked closely with decorators, builders, and the planning department to get the best deals and the quickest completion dates. Dante and Juliette were never shy in telling her how impressed they were with her work. In no time at all, the *Love & Joy* team felt like a family, leaving Juliette to go home every night with a smile on her face to the point her cheeks hurt.

The family feel was extended to Emma, too. The clients loved that while *Love & Joy* was a business, family always came first. But what surprised and warmed Avery's heart the most was how Milo – Juliette's son – had naturally fallen into the role of Emma's babysitter. He was wonderful with her, and as the months went by, he adopted the role of big brother. It was beautiful. Avery couldn't remember a time when she was so happy.

Love & Joy gave Avery the perfect work-life balance. On the days when she knew she needed a break, she could work from home and hire a babysitter to help with Emma while still having a hand in her day-to-day life. She grew close to Dante and Juliette, and with the help of Milo, she was able to go out and make new friends in Summershore.

Four

"Hey guys, guess what?" Avery cheered after ending her phone call.

"What's up?" Dante asked.

"The speed dating event I'm organizing for *Love Online* just called, and they said it's proving to be even bigger than expected. They have a few open slots and asked if any of the team wanted to join. I said I would ask and get back to them. What do you think? I'm game. Who else?" Avery asked.

"It might be fun. Sign me up!" Dante shouted, already hyper about the idea.

"I don't know," Juliette mumbled.

"Oh, go on, Mom. It will be fun," Milo interjected

"Exactly, it will be fun. We don't even have to take it too seriously. I'm not looking for anything serious right now, but who wouldn't want to be wined and dined and treated to a date every once in a while?" Avery spoke up, trying to convince Juliette.

"I'm just not ready for that kind of thing."

"I'm signing you up. You never know. You might change your mind and enjoy it," Avery told Juliette, jumping back to her desk, and typing the email reply.

The speed dating event wasn't for another few weeks, but Dante and Avery grew more and more excited as it drew closer. They spent days shopping for outfits and gossiping over their morning coffee about what their perfect partner would look like.

"I want tall, but not too tall. He can't be taller than me. Blonde with blue eyes. I'm partial to a tattoo. Sweet, sensitive, but also tough and manly...." Dante was positively swooning.

"You don't want much, do you?" Avery joked, shaking her head at his list of must-haves.

"I have high standards, darling. Have you seen this prize?" Dante asked, giving a mock twirl. "This king deserves a king!" Dante laughed.

Avery couldn't argue. Dante was one of a kind. He was kind, sweet, funny, and one of the most intelligent people Avery had ever met. He had a skill with people, reading them better than they could read themselves. He was terrific with Emma and was always able to cheer everyone up. The room lit up every time he walked in. He was a positive ray of sunshine that everyone needed in their lives.

"What about you?" Dante asked.

"I just want someone I have something in common with but is still their own person. Obviously, someone good with kids, who will be good for Emma and me."

"Can you be a bit more specific?" Dante enquired.

"I honestly haven't given it much thought. I thought I knew what I wanted with Gemma, but now, I'm not overthinking it and just want to let love find me," Avery answered.

The speed dating event finally rolled around. And thanks to a little helpful probing from Milo, Juliette agreed to join them. Dante jumped at the opportunity to give everyone a makeover, and the night was, all in all, a huge success. It had been set up as a networking event and a way for *Love Online* to launch itself to the public. Avery loved people-watching, and she loved watching all the singles couple up. She could tell when someone was trying to hide the fact that they liked the person in front of them. She knew Juliette wasn't entirely on board with the event, so she tried to keep a close eye on her. At least that was the plan until Steve sat down.

"Hi, I'm Steve. What's your name?"

"Avery." She offered her hand to shake.

Avery believed you could tell a lot about someone by their handshake, and Steve's was strong, firm, but tender. He was a little shorter than Avery but took care of himself. He was stylish and had dreamy brown eyes that Avery felt she could get lost in.

Out of all the people she chatted with at the event, Steve was the only one to leave a real impression. At the end of the event, Avery, Juliette, and Dante chatted at the bar, comparing their experiences.

"Thank you so much for convincing me to come tonight. I had a lot of fun," Juliette said, accepting her cosmopolitan cocktail from the bartender.

"Did anyone catch your eye?" Avery asked.

"No, I didn't feel that spark, but it has opened my eyes. I'm ready for new love. But I'm taking a leaf from your book Avery. I'm going to let love find me." Juliette smiled, clicking her cocktail glass with Avery's

"Yes, girl. I'm so happy for you!" Avery couldn't have hoped for more. Her beautiful boss had been grieving for too long. She turned towards Dante, anxious to find out his impressions of the event. "So Dante, tell us about that yummy piece of man-candy we had to drag you away from," Avery teased.

"His name is David, but I'm calling him Dave. He's cool with it. He is a dentist and fine as hell," Dante gushed, making the group laugh.

"What about you?" Juliette asked, poking Avery in the shoulder.

Avery laughed, noting how tipsy Juliette was getting. She had been so tense for months. It warmed Avery's heart to see her finally relax and let her hair down. Juliette wasn't just her boss. She had become a close friend who Avery cared for a lot.

"Excuse me?" interrupted Steve tapping Avery on the shoulder before she could answer Juliette.

"Oh hey, Steve, what's up?"

"I had a lot of fun tonight, but I had the most fun in the five minutes I spent with you. Here is my cell. call me sometime." Steve winked, placing a soft, gentle kiss on Avery's cheek before excusing himself to re-join his group of friends at the other side of the bar.

"Oh, my god, girl!" Juliette cheered.

Steve and Avery went on a few dates. He was a barista at *The Golden Coffee Bean* and joked how he had served Avery many times, but she had never noticed him. He made Avery laugh so much her sides hurt. Sadly, after date three, it became apparent that while they had fun together, they were not a good fit. They ended their dating streak amicably and agreed to stay friends. Avery never believed a word of it. In her experience, anyone who said they wanted to 'stay friends' generally disappeared completely after a month or two. However, Steve proved to be different, and even months later, they were still good friends.

"Hey Avery, are you still dating?" Steve asked one morning when Avery came to collect *Love & Joy*'s coffee order.

"No one is in the cards. Why?"

"I may have found someone who is perfect for you. Her name is Emily. Is it cool if I give her your number?"

"I don't know. I don't do blind dates," Avery hedged.

"Oh, come on. You trust me, right? Look," Steve pulled out his phone and brought up a picture of Emily.

She was cute, a short, redheaded girl with green eyes, high cheekbones, and a butterfly tattoo on her collar bone.

"Ok, fine, get her to call me," Avery reluctantly agreed with a cheeky smile. She gave Steve a quick peck on the cheek, she collected the coffee and headed out, telling herself she wasn't getting her hopes up over a blind date.

Emily turned out to be fun, but there was an age gap that Avery couldn't get past. Emily was five years younger than Avery and was still finding her place in the world. She came on a bit too strong, constantly texting and calling when Avery didn't reply right away. It was a little too much to take sometimes. Emma was always the priority for Avery, and Emily was not someone Avery thought would be a good fit in her daughter's life.

"How's dating life going?" Dante asked, after a week or two.

"I'm cooling dating for a while. Steve was nice, but we are better as friends, and Emily was just.... wow, she's sweet, but she's still a kid and isn't ready for an adult relationship. I'm just going to concentrate on Emma and work for the time being."

"Oh, sweetie," Dante hugged Avery, giving her a sympathetic look.

"It's fine. Honestly." Avery really was speaking the truth. Dating wasn't something she was ready for yet.

Not long after the dating event, Juliette met Damian, a handsome single father wanting a party for his little girl. Dante and Avery had comforted Juliette when Damian's toxic ex-girlfriend came back on the scene trying to break up their relationship. After such a rocky start, it was a pleasure to see how their relationship blossomed and strengthened after that.

Watching Dante and David's relationship develop and noticing how Juliette received so many flowers from Damian at the office, Avery was surrounded with more love than ever. Usually, she would be happy with that, but it slowly began to feel suffocating. She would go home every night alone, longing for what her friends had. But the idea of dating and opening up to someone new terrified her. That kind of relationship meant opening up about her past, and she really wasn't ready to go there again. She still had to stop herself from messaging Gemma several times a day, even though Avery knew it was a bad idea.

No, she wanted someone to share her highs and lows with. Someone who she could grow with. She missed cuddling up on the sofa, watching movies, and making plans for the future. She wasn't lonely exactly. She simply missed having that special connection with someone who saw you in a world where it was easy to get lost in the crowd.

Five

AVERY APPRECIATED HOW MUCH DANTE, Juliette, and Milo cared for her and seemed to notice when she wasn't herself. She held back though from telling them what she'd been thinking lately. Until she figured out what she wanted, she decided to play her cards close to her chest.

Love & Joy helped organize several LGBTQ+ events, and Avery was a huge part of a stunning Valentine's Day double wedding for twin brothers who married two best friends. The brides celebrated officially becoming sisters, and the couples held so much love for each other, it was dazzling. When Avery got home after the wedding, she curled up in bed with a cup of hot chocolate and loaded up *Love Online*. Working on the speed dating event had given Avery confidence in the site, so she signed up for online dating.

Avery had never tried online dating before. She found as her inbox filled with message requests, it gave her a slight sense of validation. It was a small confidence boost that she didn't know she needed. Unfortunately, most of the messages were anticlimactic. A few started with the standard *'Hi, how are you? You're hot!'* but no replies after that. A few were far too forward or demanding. She even received the odd inappropriate picture. From the tons of messages she received, only a handful resulted in any genuine conversation, and even fewer resulted in actual dates.

One date she went on was with a woman named Samantha. But when she found out that Avery had a daughter, Samantha clammed up. When Avery got home, she found Samantha had blocked her number. The next date she went on was with Eva, who was far too self-obsessed for Avery's liking. Hoping for the third time lucky, Avery agreed to go on a date with Chelsea. The conversation had flowed freely online, but it was stunted and dry in person. The evening seemed to last forever, with many awkward minutes of silence and dead-end conversations.

After all her bad luck on the dating scene, self-doubt began to creep in. She couldn't take the highs and lows. It was like a rollercoaster. The excitement of meeting someone new, the nerves about opening up, and the lows when they ghosted or blocked her were exhausting.

Online dating is not for me.

Cancelling her membership to *Love Online*, Avery closed her laptop and went to bed, but sleep didn't come easy. For the first time since the night Gemma left, her bed had never felt so empty.

The following day, Avery allowed herself to slip into a place of self-pity to the point where she couldn't even find the will to give herself her morning pep talk. Dante had texted asking if she could pick up the team's coffees while he headed out of town for a meeting about the extension of the business. Avery agreed and called her babysitter to take Emma for the day. She didn't want Emma to pick up on her bad mood. Once the sitter arrived, Avery kissed Emma goodbye and drove down to The Golden Coffee Bean.

She was struggling to carry the large order. Avery had just made it back to her car when she heard a woman groaning and complaining. Curiosity took hold, and Avery looked around, searching for the location of the commotion.

"Stupid piece of crap!" yelled a tall brunette as she kicked her car tire.

Avery knew a little about cars. Gemma had been a mechanic, bikes being her thing, but Avery had picked up a thing or two over the years. The car's hood was open, and a heap of steam poured out. The woman crouched on the ground in front of her broken-down car with her face in her hands.

Her beauty instantly struck Avery. Large, almond-shaped brown eyes, high cheekbones, and a sharp jawline gave the stranger an exotic beauty. She had a full sleeve tattoo on her left arm, a nose ring, and her eyebrow was pierced. She gave off a rock chick vibe that Avery loved.

"Need a hand?" Avery asked.

The woman jumped, not realising Avery was standing by. Jumping to her feet, she brushed off her clothes which were covered in paint spatter.

"You don't happen to know anything about piece of crap cars, do you?" she asked.

Avery laughed. "I do, actually."

Avery moved to check the engine and dropped to the ground to confirm her suspicions. Looking under the car, she saw what she needed to know. Brushing herself off, she stood up and turned to the annoyed rock chick.

"Do you want the good news or the bad news?" Avery asked.

"Good news. Always start with good news."

"I'm friends with the guy who owns the auto shop and can help you out with a deal to get this fixed."

"And the bad news?"

"Your radiator is busted. Even with a friend's discount, it will be pricey," Avery offered.

The rock chick sighed and ran her hands through her hair, kicking her tire a few more times in frustration. When she was done, she glanced over at Avery with a rueful look. "Right, all the anger is out now. Thanks for your help. I'm not going to lie. I didn't expect someone as glamorous as you to know anything about cars."

"Looks can be deceiving." Avery smiled.

"So, if you are helping me out with a friend's discount at the auto shop, it's only fair you know my name. Hi, I'm Sarah." She smiled, offering a paint and ink-covered hand to shake.

When their hands met, Avery felt her skin tingle all the way up to her elbow, "Avery." She smiled back, hoping like crazy that her interest in the other woman was obvious.

Avery called Frank at the auto shop and agreed to wait with Sarah until the tow truck arrived. She enjoyed her company. They made small talk, laughed, and joked, and Sarah flirted a lot. Avery was surprised by how much she blushed and didn't know how to react. Everything with Sarah felt so natural like they had known each other for years. When Frank came, he agreed to offer Sarah a fifteen percent discount on her repairs.

"So, how much more flirting do I need to do before you ask me for my number?" Sarah asked with a wink.

Stunned, Avery fell silent, almost dropping her phone.

"Tell you what, how about I give you mine?" Sarah chuckled, taking Avery's phone from her hand, and saving her number for her.

She hit dial and saved Avery's number in return. Winking back at her as she climbed into the truck alongside Frank and headed off to get her car fixed, leaving Avery to head back to *Love & Joy* with an ear-to-ear smile on her face.

"You're late. Everything okay with Emma?" Juliette asked, grabbing the coffee tray off Avery before she dropped it all.

"Yeah, sorry, I.... bumped into someone. Her car had broken down, and I waited until Frank came," Avery answered.

"You met someone?" Juliette chimed.

"No."

"Did you exchange numbers?"

Avery blushed, causing Juliette to chuckle softly.

"Good for you, love," she said and smiled.

Six

Avery chose to keep Sarah her little secret for now. She wanted to find out if it would develop into something before revealing anything to her friends. The day after Sarah's car broke down, she waited outside *The Golden Coffee Bean*, hoping to bump into Avery. Avery couldn't help but smile when she saw Sarah outside holding a bouquet of flowers in one hand, a cup of coffee in the other.

Sarah smiled. "Morning, I was hoping to run into you here."

"Everything okay with your car?"

"It's going to be a day or two, but yes. I wanted to thank you in person. It's so impersonal over text. You didn't have to help me, and I appreciated it," Sarah said, handing Avery the flowers.

"Oh, you didn't need to do that. I was happy to help. We girls have to stick together, right?"

After chatting a little longer, they both went about their day. Sarah kept Avery pleasantly distracted with cute texts throughout the day, and within a week, a date was arranged. For the first time in a long time, Avery wasn't dreading the first date. She liked Sarah and looked forward to getting to know her better.

"Milo, can I ask a favour?"

"Sure, Avery," Milo answered.

"I have a date tomorrow night, but I want to keep it on the DL. Are you okay babysitting Emma for a while? I'll pay you, of course."

"You don't need to pay me. You're family." Milo grinned and winked. "And don't worry. Your secret is safe with me."

Sarah and Avery arranged to go to a cocktail bar outside Summershore called *Straws and Umbrellas*. It was a hip little spot paying homage to '90s pop culture. Avery opted for a black and red floral, V-neck cocktail dress, and killer red high heels. She sat at the bar nervously waiting, nursing her vodka martini, until she saw Sarah walk in. Sarah looked beautiful in red and black plaid cigarette pants with a black studded belt. She wore a black lace bodysuit underneath, a black cropped leather jacket, and black suede platform heels that elongated her stunning legs.

"Wow, now I feel overdressed." Avery smiled, climbing down from her stool to hug Sarah.

"You look stunning," Sarah replied, kissing Avery on both cheeks, in a way that felt foreign and exotic, but very right.

Sarah ordered a beer, and instantly, the night flowed beautifully. They got along like old friends. It should have been perfect, but Avery still held a small part of herself back. She wanted to know how serious Sarah was about dating before opening up. Was this a casual thing or something more?

They discussed music, movies, food, fashion, work, and other first-date lines of conversation before Sarah decided to take the lead. "So now all the fun chat is out the way, let's get serious," Sarah said, ordering another round of drinks.

"You first," Avery said nervously.

"Ok. Well, I was born and raised in New York. I lived there all my life. I started my graffiti art career at a modern art gallery called G-A-Art. I worked there for...three years. After a major art show, probably the biggest in the gallery's history, since they were fairly new when I joined, things changed."

"How so?"

"Money grew tight, and the owner decided to stop paying me for my work. I agreed at first, believing all his lies about it just being a bump in the road. I started spending my own money on promotions, supplies, everything. Eventually, I called him on his crap and when he got angry, I left. I tried opening my own gallery. I even tried joining others, but he had connections and started derailing my career."

Avery gasped. "That's terrible!"

"It's all good. That's when I moved here. Best move I ever made. I have my own studio here, and my art is selling in galleries here, in neighbouring towns, and online." Sarah smiled.

"That explains all the paint and ink the first day we met," Avery joked.

"I can show you my studio later tonight if you like," Sarah mentioned, a spark of excitement in her eyes as she waited for Avery's response.

"That would be great. I'd love to see it."

Hearing about Sarah's issues and what made her move from her beloved New York to Summershore, Avery decided to share her story, or at least a small part of it anyway. Avery didn't like to admit it, but she had a hard time trusting people. It took her a while to allow herself to be truly vulnerable with someone.

"I moved to Summershore not long ago. Emma was only four months old. She's now almost one now. Wow.... Where has that time gone?" Avery wondered and shook her head.

"Emma?"

"My daughter." Avery paused, watching Sarah closely. How would she react?

Sarah grinned back; sensing Avery was guarded, she waited for her to continue at her own pace. Opening up, Avery explained the troubles she and Gemma had finding the right adoption agency, and bringing Emma home. She told her how things had changed between them then, and how she had come home one day to find Gemma had up and left.

"That sucks. It's her loss because I think you are amazing," Sarah offered.

"Thanks." Avery shrugged. "After she left, she filed for divorce with no warning. It was the final straw. Once everything was finalised and I realised that Gemma had given full custody of Emma over to me, I packed up and moved here. It was the best thing I could possibly have done because that's when I found *Love & Joy*."

"Who are they?"

Avery laughed and explained the business and how Dante, Juliette, and Milo had accepted her and brought her and Emma into their family. She sang their praises and made a mental note to remind them how much she appreciated their constant love and support. When she finally stopped, she looked up to find Sarah beaming at her.

"You speak about them with so much passion and love. It's beautiful."

Finishing their drinks, they headed out to call a cab. Sarah took Avery to her studio tucked in the hills overlooking the lake with a breathtaking view of the Summershore skyline. One wall housed floor-to-ceiling windows, and the other three were painted with a mix of graffiti art. One wall depicted the sunset over the skyline, and the others looked like a visual representation of all of Sarah's emotions. It was raw and vulnerable and beautiful.

Avery felt honoured that Sarah was showing this to her. She talked her through her latest pieces and showed her a large canvas she was getting ready to ship. Before the night ended, Sarah handed Avery a small canvas. When she opened the brown protective paper, Avery was stunned. Inside was a picture of her in front of Sarah's broken-down car, only Avery was dressed as a valiant warrior. In small writing across the top, it was the words, *'My knight in shining armour.'*

"Sarah, this is.... wow.... I can't thank you enough. It's beautiful. No one has ever done anything like this for me," Avery said, overwhelmed with emotion by such a beautiful and heartfelt gesture.

"You could give me a good night kiss," Sarah suggested and winked.

Seven

THE FOLLOWING MORNING, Avery arrived at *Love & Joy* with a spring in her step. As she worked, she sang along with the radio in the office a little louder than usual. Her excitement ran over into every aspect of her life. She was more enthusiastic with each event she helped organize. Dante and Juliette both enquired as to what had her so giddy, but with it being early days with Sarah, she kept her mouth closed. Only Milo truly knew the reason for the lift in her mood.

"So, how are things going with you and Damian? He seems to be a permanent fixture around this place," Avery said, eager for a change of subject before she spilled the beans about her date with Sarah.

"Wonderful," Juliette sighed.

"They are talking about moving in together," Milo offered.

"No way! Juliette, that amazing," Dante chirped, clapping his hands in applause at the announcement.

"I think it's a cause for after-work celebration drinks," Avery cheered, in the mood for celebration already.

Juliette laughed and agreed. After all the issues with Nia trying to cause conflict and almost splitting Juliette and Damian up, it was nice to see they were making moves in the right direction.

"What about David?" Avery swivelled her desk chair to ask Dante.

"Dave!" Dante jokingly snapped. He had grown quite attached to the shortened version of his new beau's name. "Things are going well. We're having fun, but you know me. I'm too old for all that lovey-dovey stuff."

Avery laughed. "Lovey-dovey stuff? Dante, you work for a wedding planner."

"It's nice planning it for *others*. I'm just enjoying things with Dave as they are," Dante offered, clearly not wanting to go into much detail.

Avery respected that. She wasn't willing to push the issue, especially since she wasn't willing to open up about Sarah yet herself.

Leaving the relationship talk behind, the conversation swiftly shifted back to business. With Avery and Dante both working hard, the company was running smoothly. The expansion had been a success; giving more space for different events while separating corporate from personal events. Avery bit her lip as she considered voicing an idea that had been on her mind more and more lately. As she looked over the accounts and saw how business was progressing and the ever-growing waiting list of clients, she knew it was time to speak up.

"Juliette, have you ever thought of franchising the business? Venturing out into the big cities? With the way business is booming, you could do that in a year or two," Avery offered.

"Wow, do you really think so?" Juliette asked, surprised.

"Of course, it would bring in a whole new revenue line, and you could spread your brand of *Love & Joy* further afield. Who knows, in the next ten years, there could be a *Love & Joy* in every state."

Juliette's expression was a mix of surprise and horror. Avery worried that she had overstepped herself. She was so enthusiastic about the business and her friend's success that she wanted to help out more, just as Dante had. The company's first expansion was his idea, and Juliette had welcomed it with open arms. A thought occurred to Avery that maybe if she were better prepared and offered Juliette her ideas with a solid business plan as Dante had, then perhaps her ideas would be taken seriously.

Juliette laughed nervously. "Slow down, Avery!"

Avery nodded, chastened. She'd definitely gone about it all wrong. "I'm sorry. I didn't mean to overstep."

"No, no, sweetie, you haven't. It's just a little scary thinking about it, that's all. But I will give your ideas some thought. I love how you and Dante care about the future of the business. It means a lot." Juliette smiled.

Eight

THE WONDERFUL THING about Sarah being a graffiti artist meant that she had the freedom to make her own hours. So, over the following months, they worked date night around Avery's schedule. They enjoyed trying new things, so they changed it up each week. Sailing on the lake, horseback riding in the hills, art classes – more for Sarah to show off her skills – pottery classes, cooking classes, the regular dinner and drinks, and the occasional movie.

The closer Sarah and Avery became, the harder it became for Avery to say goodnight. She found each time the date ended, she was left feeling deflated, wanting more. She missed her when she was gone and couldn't wait to see her again. Finally realising how she was starting to feel about Sarah, she decided now was a good time to reveal to everyone about her secret dates.

She arrived at work and waited for everyone to settle in after the morning meeting. After every morning meeting, they would gather for coffee and gossip about their lives before the day started. The only thing that was different about that particular morning was that Sarah had arrived with coffee for everyone, just as Dante unlocked the front door.

"Good morning, welcome to *Love & Joy*. How can we help you?" welcomed Dante.

"I'm here to introduce myself. I'm...."

"Sarah?" Avery walked in, recognising her voice. She took a deep breath as she turned to make the introductions. "Guys, this is Sarah. We have been dating for the last five months now."

"Well, you kept that quiet," Juliette teased, her eyes wide in surprise.

"Come in, darling, take a seat, tell us all about you," Dante insisted, helping Sarah with the coffees, and leading her over to the sofas.

"I've heard so much about you guys. I feel like I know you already," Sarah smiled, settling in next to Avery.

Dante and Juliette cooed when the couple interlocked fingers.

Sarah and Avery continued to tell them the story of how they met and how each date had gone since. Sarah told them a little about herself. That's when Avery revealed that Milo had known since date one, which made Dante and Juliette fall over laughing. Neither of them knew Milo could keep a secret.

"Wait, are you Sarah Sunny?" Milo gasped as he joined them, pushing Emma in her stroller from her morning walk.

"One and the same."

"Oh wow, Avery. When you said she was an artist, I never knew you meant Sarah Sunny. I've been a huge fan of your work since your first piece with G-A-Art," Milo enthused.

"It's always nice to meet a fan."

"Yeah, Dad took me to New York with him once on one of his business trips, we stumbled upon the gallery by accident, but it was a pretty cool night," Milo said.

"Well, while we are all getting acquainted, Sarah, there is someone I would like you to meet," Avery said, getting up and heading to her daughter.

Scooping Emma up in her arms, the little girl giggled and laughed, smiling at her mother.

"This is the most important person in my life. Emma. My daughter," Avery said.

Emma stretched out her hands towards Sarah, who took the hint and scooped the little child from Avery's arms. Seeing how much Emma responded to Sarah was the sign that Avery needed. It was time for her to tell Sarah the rest of her story. As clients arrived for their meetings,

Sarah wished everyone well, and Avery arranged to meet her for a date at lunch. Sarah agreed, as long as she brought Emma along, which pleased Avery greatly.

At lunch, Avery walked down the street, ecstatic that she had finally introduced Emma to Sarah and that it had gone so well. They decided to meet at Veggie Delight, a new Vegan restaurant that opened only a few weeks prior. Sarah spent most of their date with Emma in her arms. Emma had taken to Sarah as quickly as she had to Milo.

"I'm so happy I finally got to introduce you two," Avery smiled as Emma shook her rattle. "I'm sorry it took so long."

"Don't worry about it. I get it. She's your daughter. You don't want to introduce just anyone to her," Sarah reassured her.

"I.... Sarah.... You know I like you, right? I mean really like you. I might even go as far as saying, I...." Avery struggled with the words and blushed when she couldn't get them out.

"I love you too," Sarah interrupted with a wink laughing as Avery visibly relaxed.

The first time, saying the L-word was always a hard thing to do. After that, it flowed as freely as air.

"Yes, and it's because I love you that I want to tell you something. You have to understand. I have only waited this long because of how others have taken the news in the past. I only reveal this to people who mean a lot to me," Avery began.

"Okay," Sarah said, tucking Emma back into her stroller, giving Avery her undivided attention.

"I am Trans-gender. I was born...."

Sarah stopped her instantly, sensing how scared Avery was anticipating her reaction. Sarah slowly smiled, taking Avery's hands in hers and waiting for Avery to look her in the eyes.

"Can I ask you something?"

Avery nodded nervously.

"Are you happy? The way you are now? Is this the person you want to be?"

"Yes. I feel right. I feel complete. This is me," Avery answered.

"Who we are isn't about our gender; it's who we are in our hearts. I love you, Avery, and as long as you are happy with you, and who you are, then so am I."

"You are truly amazing." Avery smiled, pulling Sarah into her embrace.

Sarah winked. "Well, I try."

Nine

SLOWLY OVER THE FOLLOWING WEEK, Avery noticed a change in Sarah. Her texts grew less frequent, and when Avery would call, she would make excuses to hurry off the phone. She was either busy with work or had to pop out of town for two days. At first, Avery didn't think anything of it. A big Gallery in L.A. had recently approached Sarah to host their next event. It only made sense that she would throw herself into work. Avery was super happy for her. The exposure would be excellent for her career.

But by the end of the second week, Avery got a twisting feeling in her gut. *Was there more to it*? Avery fretted. Had Sarah accepted Avery's news as easily as she had admitted? Avery didn't want to get in her head too much because she knew she would freak herself out worrying over what was potentially nothing. Instead, she decided to call and see how Sarah was doing.

"Hey baby, how are you? How is work?"

"It's good. Super busy," Sarah replied dryly.

"I can imagine. Do you have any free time over the next week? When is the big event? Need any help?" Avery asked.

"I got it, thanks. Yeah, super busy. I don't know what's going on. I'll get back to you, though. How about we meet for coffee Thursday morning?"

"That sounds great. Well, I will stop distracting you. Enjoy your day. Don't work too hard. I love you,"

"Love you too," Sarah said quickly, ending the call.

With a date set for two days later, Avery relaxed a little. She told herself that she didn't need to worry after all. It was natural to be nervous after revealing a part of yourself to someone new, especially after being vulnerable enough to let someone in your heart and admit that you love them.

On Thursday morning, Avery decided to arrive at *The Golden Coffee Bean* a little early to get coffee and breakfast ready for Sarah to arrive, knowing how busy she was with her art. As the vintage clock on the wall ticked past the hour they were to meet, Avery got that sinking feeling again. She called and texted and received no reply or answer. Deciding to give up, she left Sarah's coffee and croissant on the table and headed to *Love & Joy* with Emma.

Three hours later, Sarah texted apologizing, but Avery was too upset to reply. She wanted to talk about how she was feeling with Dante or Juliette, but with a wedding, a birthday, and a business conference to organize, everyone was too busy to stand around and chat. A part of Avery was glad for the distractions. Keeping herself busy with work stopped her from overthinking and creating scenarios in her head that had her stomach spinning. Still, that didn't stop her from checking her phone constantly throughout the day.

Another week passed, and Avery eventually gave up trying to contact Sarah. Disheartened, she struggled with the feeling of heartbreak. She had revealed the most vulnerable side of herself to Sarah and confessed her love. And since then, she had hardly seen her. She wanted to believe that Sarah wouldn't just up and leave, especially not after Avery told her about how Gemma left. But everything felt all too familiar.

Heading to work one morning, Avery stopped dead in her tracks when she spotted Sarah waiting at their favourite table outside *The Golden Coffee Bean*, two coffees and croissants waiting. Anger roiled through Avery. Her jaw clenched. She couldn't believe Sarah would ignore her attempts to reach out and turn up as though nothing had happened. She decided to ignore Sarah and walk right by.

That didn't work.

"Avery, baby. I'm so happy to see you. Hi, Emma, how are you, sweetheart?" Sarah asked, kneeling to Emma's level and pinching her chubby cheek.

"Are you?" Avery asked, her voice tight.

"Excuse me?"

"Happy to see me? You have been avoiding me for weeks, and now you show up like nothing has happened." Avery felt her anger growing until her hands shook. She was glad to have the handle of the stroller to cling to.

"I know, I'm sorry. I handled all this wrong. Please sit and have coffee. I've missed you."

"I'm late for work, and I don't have time for liars."

"Liars? What the hell, Avery?" Sarah snapped.

"You told me you loved me and then acted the same way Gemma had. You don't do that to someone you love," Avery snarled, pushing past Sarah.

"Avery?.... Avery?" Sarah called after her as Avery rushed off to work, trying to ignore her shaking hands and the tears threatening to fall.

Avery had time to calm down and reflect as she replied to emails, typed up invoices, and checked the accounts. In hindsight, she could have handled things with Sarah differently. She wondered if she'd given up on things forever. She didn't mean to call Sarah a liar. She had let her emotions run away with her. She wished she had given Sarah a chance to explain before snapping. But Avery was a stubborn person and didn't want to be the first to reach out.

Throughout the rest of the day, she held to this resolve. Even as she grew frustrated waiting for a text or call from Sarah, she dug in her heels, telling herself that she would call when she was good and ready.

Ten

MUCH TO AVERY'S SURPRISE, Sarah turned up at *Love & Joy* just before closing. Clients were still in the office. Avery hadn't told anyone about Sarah becoming distant or the argument at the coffee shop that morning. Her heart pounded when she saw the annoyed look creasing Sarah's brow.

"Hi Sarah, are you looking for Avery?" Juliette asked.

"Yeah, is she here?"

Avery stormed from her desk, pulling Sarah to a small corner tucked away from the clients by the front door.

"You turned up at my work? I love these people, but they do not need to see us argue. This is so over the line," Avery whispered angrily.

"Over the line? You called me a liar and then stormed off. I want to talk about this," Sarah replied, drawing herself up to meet her gaze with a hint of defiance and something else Avery couldn't quite define.

"Not here."

"Then were Avery? You stormed off. Let me speak," Sarah pleaded.

"Outside," Avery snapped, storming out the front door, not looking back to see if anyone was watching.

Sarah swiftly followed Avery around the building to the one wall with no windows for clients or co-workers to peek out of.

"Talk," Avery said stiffly, crossing her arms defensively over her chest.

"Me? What about you? I admit I shouldn't have distanced myself. I should have been honest and said I was a little taken back by your news. For that, I will apologize. I'm not an unreasonable person. Are you going to admit you were wrong in calling me a liar?" Sarah snapped.

Avery sighed and relaxed a little. She couldn't argue with Sarah when she had been telling herself all day that she was wrong in how she'd acted.

"I'm sorry for calling you a liar. It's how I felt. You said you love me, that you are fine with who I am, and then you stop texting, answering calls, and stand me up on our date. Like, what the hell? If you're not okay with it, just tell me."

"I'm sorry. After how Gemma left you, I should have handled things better. I struggled for a day or two, adjusting. I've never been with a trans person before, so I didn't know how to take it. I have no issue with you being trans. I stand by what I said that day. As long as you are happy with yourself, then so am I. Please, Avery, I messed up. Can we try again? I've never felt about anyone the way I feel about you. Please don't throw this away," Sarah pleaded, visibly upset.

Avery had never seen that side of Sarah. Seeing her getting upset broke Avery's heart. She didn't want to fight, she also didn't want to lose Sarah, but she didn't think she could take heartbreak again. Avery pulled her into her arms as mascara travelled down Sarah's face.

"I don't want to fight either. Let's draw a line under it. Come to my house tonight for dinner, and we will discuss everything and go from there," Avery said.

"So, are you still my girlfriend?" Sarah asked.

"If you will have me," Avery smiled.

Deciding to approach their relationship with caution, Avery decided to give Sarah a second chance, not just because she loved her but also because of Emma.

Eleven

Two years *later*

How time flies when you're having fun. Emma was almost three when Sarah and Avery agreed to try again. It took nearly losing each other to open up a line of communication. After that, Avery and Sarah decided that no matter what, it was better to be honest and risk hurting each other with the truth than hiding things and letting feelings fester to the point someone lost their cool. It turned out for the best because together they became stronger.

After Emma's second birthday, Sarah and Avery decided to look for a place big enough for all of them. It had to be close enough to Sarah's art studio and *Love & Joy*. They were in no rush. They wanted everything to be perfect.

"Hey guys, we have some news," Juliette cheered as Sarah and Avery walked into the office.

"Sit, sit." Dante insisted, struggling to contain his excitement.

"What's up?" Sarah asked, trying to keep up with Emma as she ran around the store.

"We know how busy you both have been trying to find your own place, and with Emma's third birthday approaching, we have decided to take to worry of your hands. Instead, we will plan the perfect teddy bear tea party for her and all her friends from preschool," Juliette said, placing the folder with all the information about the party on the table in front of Avery.

"You guys, this is so beautiful. Thank you." Avery almost couldn't speak around the lump in her throat. She was so overwhelmed by the show of love from her adopted family.

"House hunting is stressful enough, and we love you both so much. We wanted to do something for you," Dante hugged Sarah tightly back.

Sarah and Avery sat Emma down and looked through the folder. Juliette and Dante had thought of everything, and Avery could spot the small touches where even Milo had an input.

The party plan was so sweet. It was organized for the park with a huge gazebo. There would be a large round table decorated with a baby pink and white tablecloth, and matching chair covers. The table was decorated with multiple little tea sets, and next to each chair was a smaller one for each child's favourite Teddy bear. In addition, each child would have their own calligraphy place setting and a personalised goodie bag as a keepsake for the day.

After the tea party, there was going to be a cake styled like a teddy bear made up of a large multi-tiered bear-shaped cake and cupcakes. Entertainment would include a magic show, puppet show, and a petting zoo with a Disney princess-themed disco to end the day.

"This is so beautiful," Sarah said, her voice catching at the level of detail and thought put into the event. "You guys are so awesome."

"Well, Avery and Emma are family, and when you and Avery got together, you joined our family. So now, I will take Emma to preschool, and you two have an appointment with the realtor over on Summer-shore strip, by the lake," Milo grinned, struggling to hide the secret he was obviously keeping.

"We didn't have any viewings today," Avery said, confused, eyeing her friends with suspicion.

"Oh yes, you do. We called in a favour. Choosing a home is deeply personal, but I couldn't help myself when I saw this. You have to see it. It would be perfect for you," Dante cheered, clapping his hands in excitement.

Avery and Sarah accepted Dante's help even if they thought he may have been a touch too involved. On the drive to the address he gave them, they discussed how to thank him but politely ask him to leave them to find their home on their own.

All issues went out the window, vanishing on the breeze when they pulled up to the house tucked into the hillside. White picket fences surrounded a small garden. The porch was twice the size of Avery's, with enough space for a porch swing and dining set to enjoy breakfast in the garden. Three storeys showed off a mix of modern and gothic architecture. It was stunning.

As the realtor walked them from room to room, they fell in love with the house. The kitchen with its central island was bigger than the entire first floor of Avery's current home and opened up into a large living and dining area. A spiral staircase led to the next floor, which consisted of two bedrooms. The master had its own en suite bathroom, and the second bedroom was perfect for Emma, right next to the family bathroom. The best part was the attic, a massive space with skylight windows that framed the sky beautifully.

"Dante said this would be perfect for a private art studio," the realtor said.

Sarah turned to Avery with tears in her eyes. Avery's skin tingled with goosebumps. The house was perfect. It was everything they could have dreamed of and more.

At Emma's teddy bear tea party, while the children played, danced, and enjoyed watching their parents attempt to make balloon animals, Sarah and Avery decided to share their good news with the group.

"You put an offer in on the house?" Dante cheered with tears of joy in his eyes.

"We did, and even better, they accepted it! We move in next week," Avery answered.

"Darlings, that's amazing. I'm so happy for you," Juliette cheered, flinging her arms tightly around them both.

Looking at the joy in her daughter's eyes and the way she laughed and played with her friends, Avery was struck with a sense of gratitude. Summershore had been the best thing for her. Emma was thriving. Watching as the little girl ran excitedly over to Sarah with her blue balloon-shaped poodle, Avery was close to tears. Seeing Sarah with Emma and knowing that soon they would all be sharing a home, Avery realised it was the happiest she had ever been. Life was good and beautiful, and she couldn't want anything else.

After the tea party, Sarah carried a very tired Emma in her arms and wished everyone well, not forgetting to thank everyone for their help and kindness. Avery gave Dante, Juliette, and Milo thank you gifts. Milo received the latest video game that Avery knew he had been saving up for, and Dante was given front row tickets to the latest concert at the orchestra hall. Juliette was given a selection of things for her upcoming honeymoon with Damian. Juliette had married Damian the previous year, but with wedding season keeping everyone at *Love & Joy* busy, they had been forced to delay their honeymoon until things weren't quite so busy.

Twelve

MOVING into their new home was stressful, but Avery and Sarah welcomed the challenge with open arms. Saving each hectic night in their memories, looking at them as the first seeds in the garden that was their love.

"Diamonds are forged under pressure. All this stress is the pressure needed to make our life shine," Sarah said.

Avery laughed and kissed her. "You are so poetic sometimes."

Emma loved her bedroom, which Sarah had decorated herself. The wall behind her bed had a jungle mural painted over it with some of Emma's favourite animal cartoon characters. Avery turned out to be a dab hand with carpentry and DIY, building Emma a small stage area in the corner of her room for whenever she wanted to perform to her teddy bear audience. Avery had recently started Emma in ballet and found that she loved it, taking to it like a duck to water. The girl was a natural.

Having the loft space, Sarah sold her old studio, putting the money towards saving for the future. Together, they moved all her art supplies to the attic. Avery would spend many nights cooking beautiful dinners in the kitchen and dancing around the living room. Their little home was everything they had dreamed of and more.

"Welcome back, Mrs. .... wow, look at that tan. The Bahamas looks good on you," Avery cheered, welcoming Juliette back to *Love & Joy*.

"How was the honeymoon?" Dante asked.

"Wonderful, I almost didn't want to come back. But I couldn't leave you guys. I missed you!" Juliette sighed, smiling like a love-struck teenager.

"So come on then, now the fun part," Avery smiled.

"Fun part?" Juliette asked, confused.

"Yeah, for us. Pictures, woman, we need to see pictures," Dante cheered, placing a tray full of freshly made coffee and breakfast pastries on the table.

"Where was it you stayed again?" Dante asked, tucking into some grapes.

"Cape Santa Maria, we had our own private villa right on the beach." Juliette handed him photographs of the view from their room.

White sand beaches, sunsets over the sea. The pictures looked like heaven, but Avery's favourite photos were not of the beautiful landscapes or the sunsetting of an evening. It was the pictures of Damian and Juliette together, sharing their evening meal wrapped in each other's arms. Staring lovingly into each other's eyes and laughing.

"They say a picture speaks a thousand words; these pictures screamed a dictionary. Just so much love and beauty. What you and Damian have...it's like movie love." Avery cooed, unable to take her eyes off the images.

Juliette smiled back. "You are too sweet. I always thought that's what you and Sarah had."

Movie love, Avery thought. Every time she thought of Sarah, her heart skipped a beat. Every time she looked at her smile, her stomach filled with butterflies. Every bit of good news, every bit of bad, she wanted to share it all with Sarah. Sarah had quickly become the centre of Avery's world.

Movie love. She couldn't get the words out of her head all day. As she locked up to head home, Avery stopped, staring at the beautiful sign above the front door. *Love & Joy* was the perfect name. In its simplicity, it spoke to everything she felt about Sarah. That was when she knew what she had to do.

With Emma in bed and Avery finishing up her latest art piece upstairs, Avery took out her laptop and searched online for the perfect ring. She wanted something different because Sarah wasn't just any woman. She had a unique sense of style, one which changed day to day solely based on her mood. Avery wanted something that represented the love she felt filling her heart and the beauty Sarah had brought to her life.

Keeping a close eye on the stairs, not wanting Sarah to see what she was searching for, Avery scrolled countless websites, but nothing spoke to her. Solitaires were too obvious, and princess cuts too simple. Halo rings seemed too blingy for Sarah, but then she saw it. A yellow gold band with a black emerald cut diamond, more petite with pale pink pear-shaped sapphires on either side, and diamonds cascading down the shoulders. It was perfect and spoke to the ups and downs, the light and dark moments of their relationship. It was perfect. She clicked the reserve button and arranged a viewing of the ring the following day. She didn't want to wait. She knew that ring was *the ring* and couldn't wait to see Sarah's face.

As soon as Avery held the ring in her hand, she knew no other ring would capture how she felt about Sarah. She didn't bother to try and haggle the way she had heard so many of her clients had. Slapping down her credit card, she bought the ring on the spot.

"Your girlfriend is going to love this. How do you plan on proposing?" asked the clerk.

Avery had given it a lot of thought. Smiling back, she answered, "I'm planning a scavenger hunt. I will start by leaving her a note on her pillow to take her to the place we first met. I will ask my friend Frank who fixed her car, to hand her the next clue. Each clue will lead to another significant spot in our relationship. She'd finally end up back at home. I will have a candlelit dinner prepared, rose petals, champagne, the works."

"That is so beautiful. Congratulations."

Thirteen

AVERY WANTED the proposal to be perfect. While she felt the ring burning a hole in her pocket and wanted to scream her love for Sarah from the rooftops, she kept herself in check. She wanted their proposal story to be one that their family would talk about for years.

Every detail had to be perfect. One evening, she typed up a list of all the moments she wanted to capture in her proposal. Starting with the day they met, their first date, and *Straws & Umbrellas*, to when Sarah gave Avery her painting. She wanted the scavenger hunt to be a journey through time and showcase everything they had been through together, both the highs and the lows. She even picked the location of their first big fight, as well as the second and third, she also wanted Emma to be involved somehow because Emma meant so much to them both.

Hours later, she had her memory roadmap and began her spreadsheet of clues for each one. With each completed clue, her excitement grew. With Sarah's birthday approaching, Avery decided that would be the day she asked Sarah to be her wife. She could disguise the proposal as a birthday treat, telling her she would be hunting for presents.

Wow, I never knew I was so romantic. Avery smiled.

"What shall we do for your birthday?" Avery asked, knowing full well what she already had planned.

"I don't want to do anything. It's fine. It's not a big birthday anyway. You know us women, never wanting to admit being a year older," Sarah joked.

"Don't be silly. It's a celebration," Avery insisted.

"I said I don't want to do anything, okay? Just drop it. Besides, I'm super busy with work right now," Sarah snapped.

Avery was taken aback by Sarah's reaction. It had been a simple question, and she hadn't even fought too hard against her response. What was up with her? Avery was worried Sarah was under too much stress with work. She knew she was planning on opening her gallery. Perhaps she had taken on more than she could handle. Avery and Sarah had always been open with each other, sharing their burdens, so when Sarah became distant and distracted, Avery began to worry.

She didn't want to pry in case she pushed Sarah away, deciding instead to allow her space. It was hard to accept that she would come to her when she was ready to talk when all Avery wanted to do was shake her and beg her to tell her what was wrong.

Sarah's birthday approached. It was only two days before the big day. The more Sarah pulled away, the more Avery questioned if proposing was the right thing to do. One evening, staring at the ceiling, unable to sleep, Avery's mind flashed to the yellow envelope, the divorce papers, and the pain she'd felt when she came home to find Gemma gone. It didn't hurt anymore thinking of Gemma but imagining the same scenario with Sarah terrified Avery. Losing Sarah meant a heartbreak Avery didn't think she could survive. *I can't carry on like this. I'm going to talk to her in the morning,* she told herself before forcing her eyes shut and going to sleep.

The following morning Avery woke up in bed alone. A note on the bedside table read:

'Got a meeting in LA. I've taken Emma to preschool. See you at dinner.
S xxx'

Avery sat in her car outside *Love & Joy* for fifteen minutes, staring blankly into space. She was full of energy but was not motivated to do anything. The thought of life without Sarah felt empty. Slowly she felt her mind spiralling.

Stop it. Nothing has happened. You just bought a house together. Pull yourself together!

Avery dragged herself from her car. She tried to repeat her pep talk in her head but found the once comforting words did little to motivate her. Pushing the office door open, Avery jumped back, almost tripping, and screamed as party poppers and confetti cannons exploded around her.

"Surprise!" cheered everyone in the room.

"What the hell? You almost gave me a heart attack!" Avery gasped, clutching her hand to her chest, making everyone laugh.

After a few moments and her nerves settled, Avery's mouth fell open. The room was filled with white and pink roses. Canvases filled the walls, all painted by Sarah. Each canvas depicted different stages in their relationship. Their first date. When Sarah met Emma. Buying their first home. In the middle of the room, Sarah was on one knee under a golden balloon arch. It wasn't until Avery looked at the balloon arch again that she saw the balloons spelled out, 'Will you marry me?'

"What?.....what?....." Avery stuttered, utterly lost for words.

"Avery, you have been a light in my life I didn't know I needed until I found you. You encourage me, bring out the best in me and inspire me. You didn't just invite me into your life. You invited me into your family. This family," Sarah began, tears causing her eyes to sparkle like stars.

Juliette, Dante, Damian, Milo, and Emma huddled together, watching and waiting in anticipation.

"You are the most beautiful woman I have ever met, both inside and out. You have so much love to give. You share it with your clients every day, you share it with your family and friends, and you opened your heart and home to a child who needed it most. Words will never be enough to describe how I truly feel about you. But I hope this ring will, so, Avery Lannister.... Will you marry me?" Sarah asked, her voice cracking as the question left her lips.

Avery felt like she might pass out. Her head spun; her hands shook. Overwhelmed by the love that filled the room, the heartfelt words from Sarah, and the loving gaze from Emma as she clung to Sarah as if she, too, waited for Avery's reply. Avery realised that Sarah hadn't been pulling away after all. She hadn't been cold and distant. It had all been in her head. It was too much. Avery burst out crying and laughing at the same time.

Confusion filled the faces of everyone. Was her reaction good? Bad? No one wanted to ask.

"Yes, I will marry you.... on one condition...." Avery began as she reached into her purse, pulling out the ring and presenting it to Sarah. "If you will marry me too."

"Oh my god, this is too beautiful," Dante chirped, wiping tears from his eyes.

Sarah's smile lit up the room. "Of course, I will!"

Placing their engagement rings on each other's fingers Avery and Sarah pulled each other into a hug, sealing their betrothal with a kiss.

"Congratulations!" Everyone cheered.

"Ha! This is defiantly new; I've never seen a couple where both parties have an engagement ring before," Milo joked.

Fourteen

JULIETTE AND DANTE took over wedding planning just like they had with Emma's birthday party, but the brides insisted on having some input this time. They both had so many ideas, but one thing was for sure: They wanted a wedding that represented them both equally. After months of planning, too many ideas, and a few disagreements with Dante, it was settled.

They would have an outdoor wedding at the lake house. The ceremony would take place under the big blossoming oak tree with chandeliers holding small battery-operated tea lights - for safety, of course – would hang from white and black sheets of fabric draped over the larger branches. Both brides would have matching bouquets of black cilia lilies and pink roses. The reception would be decorated in a rustic theme with subtle hints of Sarah's graffiti art and rock-chick style. The centrepieces on each table would be candles framing vintage vinyl records, each one having a different song that held meaning for the happy couple. Milo thought it would be adorable to have Emma wear a pink ballerina style dress with a little leather jacket with 'I love my mommies' written across the back.

Music would be a string quartet for the ceremony and a harpist during the meal. Sarah insisted her brother's punk rock band perform a few songs later in the evening at the reception. When they were not performing, there would be a DJ. It was going to be a wedding of beauty, love, music, and art; a true representation of Avery and Sarah. One thing that Avery and Sarah insisted on was keeping their wedding outfits hidden from each other. That was the one thing they each wanted to be a surprise.

"Oh my.... this is it.... this is the dress," Avery said from behind the changing room door.

"Come on, then let me see." Juliette cheered.

Avery stepped out of the changing room in a floor-length figure-hugging modern glamour mermaid dress. Illusion lace travelled from the spaghetti straps down the plunging V-neck neckline and flowed along the bodice to the waist. The skirt trailed behind and offered a pink dip-dye effect. Avery looked magical, like a princess, bringing Juliette to tears.

"Avery.... wow, you look..."

"Bootiful mommy," Emma said, clapping her hands and jumping up and down on Juliette's knee.

Standing at the altar, Avery stood filled with nerves and excitement. Juliette was honoured when Avery asked her to be her maid of honour, and she stood by her side with pride, holding her hand. The music started, and the guests fell silent. Avery turned slowly to see Sarah, her arm linked with her dad's, gliding towards her. Emma held tight to Sarah's other hand. Sarah looked a vision in her floor-length black V-neck long-sleeved gown. The gold flowers and vine detail covering every inch gave Sarah a glamorous look. She reminded Avery of a movie star walking the red carpet.

"Do you Avery Lannister?"

"I do."

"Do you, Sarah...."

"I do!" Sarah jumped in too excited to let the officiant finish her name.

"It gives me great pleasure to pronounce you married."

The day flew by in a blur. Avery couldn't take her eyes off Sarah. The ceremony was simple, beautiful, and didn't leave a dry eye in the house. Everyone celebrated with cocktails, music, dancing, and Sarah's surprise graffiti show. At the reception, she painted a picture of the moment they'd said, "I do."

It was a wedding like no other. A wedding true to two people who were meant to be together. True love. True family. True, love and joy.

"Dante, I can't thank you and Juliette enough for organizing all this. It's magnificent." Avery smiled.

"It was an honour, my dear," Dante replied, clinking his glass in cheers.

"I haven't seen you on the dance floor."

"Ha! You won't, not will all these loved-up songs. Who would I dance with?" Dante asked.

"I did notice David isn't here. Is everything okay?"

"It's your wedding, don't you worry about me," Dante grinned, obviously trying to mask his hurt.

"Dante?"

"Alright, fine.... we split up. We are staying friends; it just wasn't meant to be. But don't you worry that beautiful face. I really am fine," Dante said, squeezing Avery's face between his palms and making her laugh.

"Love will find you one day, and I will have the honour of organizing your wedding. I promise," Avery said, hugging him tightly.

"I'm sure you will," Dante said, patting her softly on the back.

His words may have been said in agreement, but Avery was no fool. She could tell Dante was hurting and hiding it well. But she didn't want to upset him. He was a strong guy, and he knew when and if he wanted to talk, she would be there for him.

"Come, dance with me on my wedding day." Avery smiled, leading Dante to the dance floor.

Fifteen

VERONA. The home of Shakespeare's star-crossed lovers Romeo and Juliette. A place steeped in medieval architecture, rich history, art, and everything needed to celebrate Avery and Sarah's first anniversary. Juliette and Damian had kindly volunteered to look after Emma for the week, allowing the head-over-heels in love couple a much-needed break just the two of them.

When they were not enjoying the beautiful open-air markets, soaking up the beautiful city's history, and taking tours, Avery and Sarah enjoyed a new restaurant and cafe every day. They wanted to sample everything and go home with fabulous stories to tell all their friends. Sarah had taken multiple pictures for inspiration for her art when she got home, and Avery had collected a small number of souvenirs as tokens from their trip.

The year since they married had flown by so quickly, but Avery had loved every second. Sarah gasped for breath as Avery laughed. Sarah had wanted to take the elevator, but Avery had insisted on the stairs, saying they both needed the exercise after all the food they had been indulging in since they arrived. Their trip was due to end the following day, and Avery wanted to soak up as much of Italy as she could before they left.

The view over Verona from the top of the tower at Torre Dei

Lamberti was breath-taking. Buildings for as far as the eye could see, sights you could miss just walking the streets. It was a wonderful place to take a step back, breathe, and reflect.

A house. A home. A family. Avery had everything she had ever wanted. The previous year had been crazy but in the best possible way. They had moved into their home, got married, and Sarah had finally accomplished her dream of opening her own art gallery. Avery's career with *Love & Joy* had gone from strength to strength, with Juliette finally agreeing to look at opening a second store out of town. Emma was thriving and loved Sarah so much that it made Avery's heart want to burst with joy. Separately, Avery and Sarah were doing great. Together, they were an unstoppable team, and as a family, they were unbreakable.

They say that the honeymoon period fades just as quickly as it starts. But as Avery turned to look at Sarah, she realised that the old saying was a lie. Their love, spark, and flame were an inferno with no sign of burning out any time soon.

"I can't believe we are here," Avery breathed.

"What? We have been here a week," Sarah teased.

"No, silly. I mean here. Us, together. A family."

Sarah wrapped her arms around Avery's waist, hugging her tightly to her chest and resting her chin on Avery's shoulder. Snuggled tightly in her wife's embrace, the pair stood silently staring out over the beauty that was Verona, Italy. Content with just enjoying each other, the sights, the smells, and the sound of life bustling below their feet.

Reflecting was beautiful, but Avery couldn't wait to see what else the future had in store.

"I was thinking.... how would you feel about adding to our little family?" Sarah whispered in Avery's ear.

"Like a puppy?" Avery asked, her heart beating a little faster despite the playful tone.

"No....like adopting another child. Maybe a little boy," Sarah ventured.

Avery spun around to face Sarah, her skin igniting in goosebumps. Her heart felt like it was growing ten times as fast, filled to bursting.

"Are you serious?" Avery asked, trying to control the smile that stretched ear to ear.

"I've been thinking about it for a while. What do you think?"

"I love it! Let's do it!" Avery cheered.

On the plane home, watching Italy slip away and confirming their anniversary celebration was coming to an end, Avery half expected to feel the usual holiday blues. But with the prospect of adding to their family, she couldn't wait to get home. She missed Emma dearly. They both did. But she also couldn't wait to see the look on Emma's face when she found out she would be a sister.

"Hey guys, how was Verona?!" Damian asked, welcoming them both inside.

"Wonderful, we couldn't have picked a better place. I have so many ideas for the gallery. I can't wait to get back to the studio," Sarah replied.

"Mommies," came Emma's sweet voice running from the living room, closely followed by Juliette and Milo.

Avery knelt and wrapped Emma in the biggest hug she could.

"I missed you," Emma said.

"We missed you too, sweetie, but we have a surprise for you," Avery said, looking to Sarah for confirmation.

"A surprise, what is it? What is it?" Cheered Emma bouncing up and down in excitement.

"How would you feel about having a little brother?" Sarah asked, kneeling to join her family.

Emma shrieked out her excitement, wrapping her tiny arms as far around Avery and Sarah as she could before running around Juliette's hallway, cheering to everyone who would listen.

"Milo! Milo! I'm going to have a baby brother. I get to be a big sister," Emma cheered, jumping up at Milo.

"You will make an amazing big sister Emma!" Milo smiled.

"You guys are just too perfect." Juliette smiled, wiping away a tear as she smiled back at Avery.

"Congratulations, guys!" Damian grinned.

"Well, we only decided on the way home, but we will do it, and we can't wait," Sarah confirmed.

"Seeing the love you two have for each other and how wonderful you both are with Emma, it will not be long before you hold your little boy in your arms," Milo said.

"Have you told Dante yet?" asked Milo.

"No, why don't we call him now? Avery grinned, pulling out her phone and hitting the video call button.

It didn't take long for Dante to answer and even less time before he screamed so loud Emma had to cover her ears, and everyone erupted into laughter.

"Mommy, Sarah?" Emma asked, tugging on Sarah's jacket.

"Yes, sugar plum?"

"While I wait for my baby brother, can I get a kitten?" Emma asked sweetly, peering up with the biggest and cutest eyes she could muster.

"Ha, ha. What do you think, Avery?" Sarah asked.

"Sure, sweetie, we'll go to the shelter this weekend," Avery answered.

"Yay! I get a baby brother and a kitten! You are the best. I love my mommies!"

A house, a home, and an ever-growing family. Avery had everything she ever wanted, and it felt better than she ever could have imagined.

Without realising she was even looking for it, she had found home.

The End

Did you enjoy *Something Borrowed*?

Please consider rating it on Bookbub, Goodreads or your favorite retailer.

Reviews help me reach new readers.

Read *Something Blue*, the next story in *The Wedding Trio*.

Join my Newsletter for updates and giveaways at www.daisylandishromance.com!

Sneak Peak

Something Blue

Chapter 1

Dante sat and watched Sarah and Avery dancing together. The night was almost over, but the atmosphere was still electric. A tear brimmed his eyes, and his heart grew warm, sharing in their love for one another. The look on their faces when they saw the venue all decorated for the first time, the nuances and little details that spoke to them. It meant so much. It was a day they would never forget.

Dante was a hopeless romantic; he loved love. And being a part of a couple's special day meant he could experience new love all the time. Organising a wedding meant structure, organisation, lists, and every-thing Dante enjoyed to the fullest. All the things that helped him calm his mind and distract him from the shitty parts of the world.

Dante had been in love before. Several times actually. But he had yet to walk down the aisle himself. He was content in being a part of other people's big day, but he never fancied that day for himself. He never told anyone about how he felt. How could he explain that he loved love but never wanted to get married? What would his clients think if he told them that he believed it unnecessary and doomed to fail? It was ironic considering how much he loved planning weddings.

Dante loved hearing others' love stories and what brought them together, each such a different, exciting tale, pulling at the heartstrings and sparking hope. A hope that Dante would always ignore. Instead, he chose to live his life enjoying love without the pressures of finding *the one*. He looked at a wedding as a puzzle; he tasked himself with finding all the missing pieces to make the happy couple smile and bask in the result.

Weddings were beautiful, a time to bring people together, a time to share love and forget about everything else. It was the togetherness, the love that every person in the room shared that Dante loved; spreading happiness and joy was so important. In a world already so full of conflict and heartache, a wedding was the one time that all differences were put aside. And instead of tearing each other down, people wished the best for each other.

When he found the job at *Love and Joy*, it was a dream come true. A chance to enjoy that excitement and joy every day, a chance to immerse himself into organising and planning – his favourite things! And when Juliette had offered him ownership over part of the business after he helped it expand, he was over the moon. Something that was his that he could nurture and grow and help bring that feeling to others. It was his own. It was his calling.

Wedding and parties always made him feel special, like he was in the cool kid club. They made him feel light as air, like he might take off flying at a moment's notice. His footsteps would be lighter, and every day he would look forward to checking off a new task on his list; watching the seeds he had planted flourish into beautiful flowers. Every night he would go to bed with a sense of accomplishment and satisfaction. No other job he had worked before gave him that feeling.

Every cloud has a silver lining. But in Dante's experience, every sunny day had a cloud. It was that little voice of doubt in Dante's mind that made him wonder how long a marriage would last. He would watch the couples on their big day with hope and prayer that they would be back to plan an anniversary or celebrate the birth of a child in a few years. He hated it when he could tell a couple was getting married because they felt obligated to after being together for so long or because of family ties—those weddings were doomed to fail and reinforced the fact that Dante would never get married.

Dante helped plan every wedding that came through *Love and Joy*, and that little voice would ask him, *Have you done enough? Will this wedding be enough?* A small part of him wanted to believe that if the wedding was perfect, if the couple was so overwhelmed with joy and memories to remind them of why they chose to get married, then maybe, just maybe, that marriage would be a success.

Chapter 2

Dante first fell in love with weddings when he was ten; when his mother and father were getting married. His parents saved their money for years to afford their wedding. And the time had finally arrived. Dante loved seeing his mother so happy, finalising all of the details, picking out a colour scheme, and smiling as she crossed off the days on the calendar.

When the day finally came, everything was beautiful. And seeing his mother and father staring at each other with nothing but love in their eyes was perfect. As Dante grew up, he would pull out their photo album and stare at the pictures, remembering all the feelings from that day.

A couple of years later, when the arguments started and his parents spent less time together, Dante relied on that little photo album more often. Memories of a happier time. His parents didn't notice it was missing, so Dante kept it hidden under his bed for safekeeping.

One night, when he woke to hear his mother crying in the kitchen, he snuck out of bed carrying the photo album in hopes of cheering her up; his heart broke when it didn't work. The following day, he woke up to find his father was gone. He never saw him again.

It was only years later that his memory of what happened that night came back. He assumed he had blocked out the memory or dreamt it. But he hadn't.

"You trapped me! I never wanted kids; I never wanted to get

married. I did all that because I cared. And look what it's gotten me. I don't know who I am anymore, and that's because of *you*. Goodbye, Keira!" His father had screamed.

The years went by and Dante watched his mother try to replicate the love she had for his father. First came Darius, a doctor from Chicago. That marriage failed when he cheated. Next came Tom, the car salesman. That marriage ended because Tom worked too much, and Keira didn't like the lack of attention. The third was Jerry. He said that Keira was too needy. Each time, Keira had seemed happy and the wedding was beautiful. But the marriage never lasted. As Dante grew older and helped his mother while she cried, saying how she thought this one was the one, Dante realised that marriage wasn't something he ever wanted.

He loved weddings, love, and the beauty of romance. But the thought of feeling that love and comfort, only to sit there in heartbreak when it all fell apart was too much. Watching his mother search for 'the one,' and spending so much of her life searching for what she thought was the answer to all her problems only to be disappointed, he could not bear it. It was draining, and Dante didn't want to live his life like that.

With each marriage, Dante watched Keira change. She would lose a part of herself, and vice versa, her partner did as well. From what Dante knew of love, it was meant to be good and pure. It was a partnership, each person bringing out the best in the other. A partnership based on love and support, and being each other's strengths not weaknesses. What he saw of love from his mother's list of failed marriages was not love. When he got the job at Love and Joy, Keira had asked her son to plan her upcoming wedding. It had been the first wedding that Dante had refused to plan. He wanted no part in it.

Read *Something Blue*, the next story in *The Wedding Trio*.

www.ingramcontent.com/pod-product-compliance
Lightning Source LLC
Chambersburg PA
CBHW050905120626
46554CB00003B/1027